SCOOBY-DOO!

AND THE

SCARY SNOWMAN

by Mariah Balaban

SCHOLASTIC INC.

New York   Toronto   London   Auckland   Sydney
Mexico City   New Delhi   Hong Kong   Buenos Aires

visit us at www.abdopublishing.com • Reinforced library bound edition published in 2012 by Spotlight, a division of the ABDO Group, 8000 West 78th Street, Edina, Minnesota 55439. Spotlight produces high-quality reinforced library bound editions for schools and libraries. Published by agreement with Warner Bros.—A Time Warner Company. The stories, characters, and incidents mentioned are entirely fictional. All rights reserved. Used under authorization. Printed in the United States of America, Melrose Park, Illinois. • 052011• 092011

Cataloging-in-Publication Data

Balaban, Mariah, 1977-.
    Scooby-Doo! and the scary snowman / by Mariah Balaban ; cover and interior illustrations, Duendes del Sur. -- Reinforced library bound ed.
        p. cm. -- (Scooby-Doo)
    Summary: A winter ski trip turns into a scary surprise when a snowman-building contest goes awry.
    [1. Scooby-Doo (Fictitious character)--Juvenile fiction. 2. Dogs--Juvenile fiction.
    3. Snowmen--Juvenile fiction. 4. Ski resorts--Fiction. 5. Mystery and detective stories.]
    [E]--dc22
    ISBN 978-1-59961-869-2 (reinforced library bound edition)

Scooby and the gang were going on a ski trip.

"Golly, there's something for all of us at Von Schnee's Winter Wonderland!" exclaimed Velma. "Skiing, ice-skating, snowboarding . . ."

"Let's not forget smorgasbords!" Shaggy interrupted.

"Rorgos-rords?" Scobby asked.

"Yeah, good buddy, like, that's Swedish for 'eat everything in sight'!"

Finally, the gang arrived at Von Schnee's Winter Wonderland. The ski lodge was warm and cozy.

"Golly, look, there's Jack Frostfield!" exclaimed Velma. "The Olympic ski jumper and owner of the mega ski-resort chain Alpine Jack's!"

"It looks like he's talking to the Von Schnees — the owners of this place," said Fred.

"It sounds like they're having an argument!" said Daphne.

4

"You'll sell your rinky-dink resort to me if you know what's good for you!" Jack Frostfield muttered as he stormed away. The gang wanted to figure out what was going on.

Lars Von Schnee explained to the gang that Jack Frostfield wanted to buy the Von Schnee family business to expand the Alpine Jack empire.

"And we'd be fools not to take his offer!" exclaimed his brother Olaf.

"Olaf and I don't see eye-to-eye on this," said Lars. "The ski resort means the world to me. Olaf doesn't even know how to ski!"

"Let's talk about this later. It's almost time for the snowman-building contest," Olaf said as he checked his pocket watch and walked off.

"Kids, I'd be honored if you'd be my guests. Why don't you take these tickets for the contest and these coupons for the snack bar?" offered Lars.

"Like, who needs a smorgasbord when you've got a snack bar?" joked Shaggy.

Soon the snow was flying — the contestants built snowmen with amazing speed.

"The snowmen are all so realistic," said Daphne. "Why, that one in the distance looks like it's moving on its own!"

"Yikes!" exclaimed Shaggy. "Like, that's one scary snowman!"

Suddenly, a fierce wind started to blow.

"Skiers, stay off the slopes or else! The weather report calls for dangerous snowstorms!" growled the Scary Snowman.

"Jeepers!" said Daphne. "That overgrown snowball just started a blizzard!"

"And you guys say that I'm flakey!" said Shaggy. "Like, let's get outta here!"

When the snow had settled, the gang found Lars Von Schnee. "That snowman is going to ruin me!" he wailed. "I may as well sell my resort to Jack Frostfield while he still wants to buy."

"Don't worry," said Velma, "Mystery, Inc. will get to the bottom of this cold caper!"

The gang decided to split up and look for clues. Velma, Daphne, and Fred found their first clue by the bleachers. It was Olaf Von Schnee's gold pocket watch.

"That's odd," Velma said. "I didn't see him at the snowman contest."

"Looks like we've got ourselves a suspect!" said Daphne.

The gang found another clue by the ski slopes.

"Check this out, guys!" exclaimed Daphne. She had discovered a wind machine.

"That must be how the Scary Snowman made that blizzard," said Velma.

"Looks like it's controlled by a remote," added Fred.

Meanwhile, Shaggy and Scooby knew just where to start their search for clues — at the snack bar.

"Like, maybe it's just this ice cream," said Shaggy, "but it sure seems a lot colder all of a sudden."

"Ro-man!" barked Scooby-Doo. "Run ror rit!"

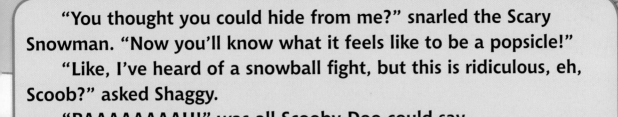

"You thought you could hide from me?" snarled the Scary Snowman. "Now you'll know what it feels like to be a popsicle!"

"Like, I've heard of a snowball fight, but this is ridiculous, eh, Scoob?" asked Shaggy.

"RAAAAAAAAH!" was all Scooby-Doo could say.

Shaggy and Scooby rolled down the hill and landed right next to the gang.

"Nice of you guys to drop in," said Velma.

"Like, that Scary Snowman just chased us down the slope on skis!" shouted Shaggy.

"On skis?" Velma asked. "Something just isn't adding up."

"Look!" said Fred. "The snowman left a set of tracks!"

The gang followed the ski tracks to a small cabin in the woods. There they found blueprints for Von Schnee's Winter Wonderland.

"Check out these blueprints! 'Von Schnee' is crossed out, and 'Alpine Jack' is written over it. I think this might be the last piece of the puzzle," said Fred. "It's time to put this snowman on ice!"

"We have to make sure he doesn't sell his lodge to Jack Frostfield!" exclaimed Daphne.

The gang rushed back to the lodge to talk to Lars Von Schnee. They arrived in the nick of time.

"You can't sign those papers!" Velma called out. "Jack Frostfield is a frozen fraud! He's been disguising himself as the Scary Snowman!"

"How can you be so sure?" asked Lars Von Schnee.

"At first I thought the Scary Snowman was your brother Olaf," continued Velma. "But the Snowman chased Shaggy and Scooby on skis, and I remembered that Olaf doesn't know how to ski!"

"How dare you accuse me!" exclaimed Jack Frostfield. "What proof do you have?"

"Proof?" asked Fred.

Right on cue, Shaggy and Scooby came speeding down the slope.

"Ahhhh!" yelled Jack Frostfield, as he flew into the air. A remote control fell out of his pocket, and he crashed with a thud to the ground.

Fred explained that Jack Frostfield used the remote to create a blizzard effect with the wind machine.

"Once he had scared all of the skiers away, he knew that the Von Schnees would sell their resort to him," Velma added.

"And I would have gotten away with it, too, if it weren't for you meddling kids and your dog!" growled Jack Frostfield as the sheriff led him away.

23

"Kids, we just can't thank you enough!" exclaimed Lars.

"To repay you, we'd like to offer you all free lifetime passes to our resort," said Olaf. "Including the smorgasbord!"

"Like, I think we'll take you up on that offer right away, ol' pal!" exclaimed Shaggy.

"Scooby-Dooby-Doo! " howled Scooby in agreement.